THE BIG BOOK OF SNOW AND ICE

Written by Štěpánka Sekaninová
Illustrated by Niké Papadopulosová

BOOK HOUSE
a SALARIYA *imprint*

Snow and ice in history and myth

Wicked people are said to have cold hearts or hearts of ice. Kind people are described as having warm, sunny dispositions. Where does our hostile attitude to ice come from?

The Ice Age

The Ice Age was a long period of cold, dry weather probably due to a change in Earth's position in relation to the Sun. Our planet has had many ice ages, the last of which ended about 8000 BCE. Although this came as a relief to shivering prehistoric humans, mammoths and woolly rhinoceroses had adapted so well that the end of the Ice Age brought about their extinction.

Niflheim

According to Viking mythology, Niflheim, a polar world of cold, mist, darkness and ice existed where there were twelve rivers of ice. Niflheim was ruled by a spiteful snake, the source of all evil. This sinister reptile was said to have wrapped itself around the Tree of Life, which it tried to destroy by gnawing at its roots.

Yuki-onna

The Japanese have Yuki-onna, a raven-haired icy demon who wears a white kimono and has snow-white skin. In snowstorms and blizzards, she entices pilgrims from their path and sometimes freezes them with her icy breath.

Snow Queen

The Snow Queen is a fairy tale by the Danish writer Hans Christian Andersen. It is about a beautiful winter queen who is the embodiment of cruelty and spite. When Gerda frees her friend Kay from the Snow Queen's clutches, the ice palace melts, spring arrives and all is well again.

Old Mother Frost

In the fairy tale, Old Mother Frost, by the Brothers Grimm, a kind old lady rules over winter. When she shakes out her quilts she covers the whole land with white down.

Santa Claus

Santa Claus also lives in a land of eternal ice and snow – but he is a kind-hearted man clothed in red and white. Each Christmas eve, he flies through the skies on a sleigh pulled by reindeer to deliver gifts to all children.

How snow originates

What is snow, actually?

Tiny particles of dust and pollen float all around us. As vapour condenses around them, raindrops form. At high altitude, where it is very cold, the raindrops freeze and become ice crystals. These crystals collide with each other and join together to become a snowflake. As they get bigger and heavier they begin to fall to the ground as snow.

Scientists estimate that since our planet came into existence, the amount of snowflakes that have fallen on it would weigh more than the planet itself. Each snowflake weighs one millionth of a gram. Can you imagine that?

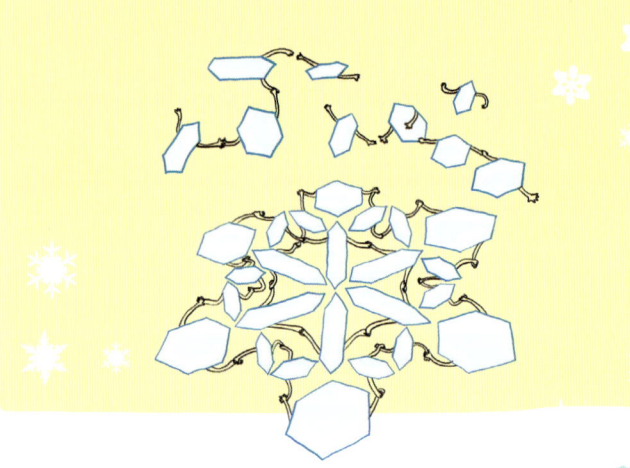

Hoarfrost

Hoarfrost is water vapour transformed into white needle-like ice crystals. This delicate structure forms around blades of grass and on the branches of trees.

A glacier

A glacier is a body of ice that is formed by the accumulation of many years of snowfall. The snow gradually gets compacted and turns into glacial ice. Glaciers are found all over the world, with the exception of Australia.

Singing snowflakes

Did you know that snowflakes 'sing' or make a sort of high-pitched squeaky sound when they fall on water? Unfortunately the human ear cannot detect it.

Totally unique

Each snowflake contains 1018 molecules of water, yet no two snowflakes in the world are the same. Each snowflake's journey down to earth affects its final shape, too.

A proper storm

In the course of a single snowstorm an average of 40 tonnes of snow fall to earth. If an African elephant weighs seven tonnes, just imagine the weight of nearly six elephants falling to ground at once!

What a whopper!

Snowflakes can be big, small, fat, thin, dry, wet – you name it! They tend to be between 0.5 cm and 1 cm in size. The biggest snowflake ever recorded – a massive 38 cm – fell in Montana, USA, in 1887.

As white as snow...

What colour is snow – white? No… snow is as transparent as a window. The edges of each crystal of snow reflect light in all directions. The human brain interprets this reflected light as white. When a car windscreen shatters, it too looks white. If snow crystals were to absorb the light rather than reflect it, snow would look black.

A good crunch

Why does snow crunch? It only crunches at temperatures lower than -2 degrees Celsius, when the ice crystals that make up the snow break. At higher temperatures, the crystals begin to thaw instead, making it slippery underfoot.

Basic types of snow

Powder snow is a fresh light-weight covering of snow that consists of large star-shaped flakes.

Fine-grained snow has lain long enough for its crystals to gradually merge into fine grains.

Wet snow is snow that is starting to thaw. If you sit on it, your bottom gets wet. But it's the best snow for building a snowman with.

Firn is snow that has partly thawed and frozen over again. It contains coarse crystals and has a layer of ice on top.

wet snow

powder snow

fine-grained snow

Ice and honeycombs

The first scientist to describe the hexagonal shape of a snowflake was Johannes Kepler, because its ice crystals reminded him of bees' honeycomb. Johannes Kepler was an eminent German mathematician, astrologer and astronomer of the late 16th and early 17th centuries.

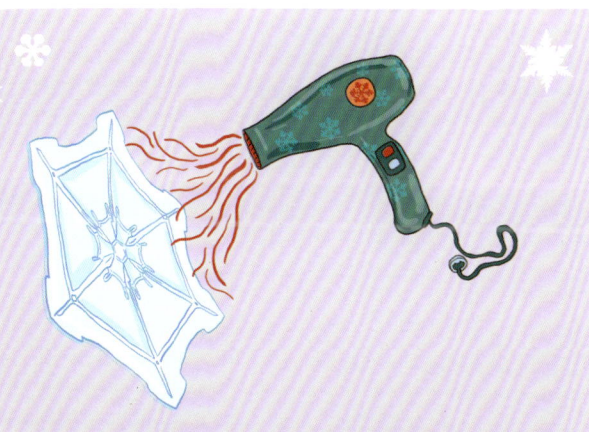

Air and snowflakes

The shape of a snowflake is determined by the temperature and the different air zones it falls through. Drier air tends to make flat shapes, while greater humidity increases volume and makes snowflakes into magnificent lace-like patterns.

Snowflakes

Magnified snowflakes look like little miracles, ice flowers, letters from the heavens… they are beautiful.

Shapes of snowflakes

A snowflake that forms in a relatively dry environment at a temperature of -15 °C is shaped like a pancake. At a temperature of around -25 °C the snowflake is shaped like a short chip. A snowflake will form into a beautiful six-pointed shape with moist air and a temperature of around -14 °C.

Nature and snow

The importance of snow

As snow falls to earth it gathers harmful dust particles. This process is important because it helps to purify the air.

Snug as a bug in a rug

A thick covering of snow is likened to a duvet for good reason – it really acts like a duvet for our planet! It protects the ground against frost penetration – just like the covers on your bed keep out the chill.

Snow protects

If frost strikes suddenly the ground freezes, making it a hostile environment for animals and plants. A blanket of snow allows small rodents and insectivores to build themselves intricate tunnel systems, where they are hidden from the eyes of predators. When there is no snow in winter, they don't have this shelter.

Flowers and snow

Snow is good for plants, too. When the ground is frozen, snow can insulate plants and protect them from harsh winds. It also helps to preserve moisture in the soil. As the snow melts it releases nitrogen and sulphur into the soil, which helps to fertilise it.

Snow keeps the temperature steady

Snow helps to regulate temperature. Although it makes it colder by day, snow also insulates the ground underneath it, a situation some animals use to their advantage. One creature that can drop its body temperature to freezing to survive the snows of winter is the frog. However, if frosts strike before there's any snow, the frost-protection systems of these animals are unable to cope with the fluctuations in temperature, and they perish.

It's a hard life in the snow and ice

Animals who live in regions with permanent snow and ice don't have an easy life. It is very difficult for them to maintain their body temperature in snowy areas. They spend a lot of time on the move, searching for food in or under the snow. Heavy snow makes this more difficult and takes a great deal of energy.

Winter sleepers

Fluctuations of temperature are not good for hibernators, such as dormice and ground squirrels. In order not to freeze to death, their body temperature should never fall much below zero. A covering of snow can insulate or help maintain temperatures below it.

Natural waterworks

Mountain ranges form a natural waterworks system. Snow accumulates in the mountains over the winter months and eventually turns to water in the spring-time thaw. The melting snow provides water for many miles around.

Polar bear

"Hi! I'm used to eternal winter. My white coat blends in so beautifully with the snow that I'm almost impossible to spot. Each hair of my white fur is hollow, and is full of air. The air keeps me warm and carries me high in the water when I swim. Perhaps you humans copied this idea from my fur? Just think of the hollow fibre in your winter jackets and sleeping bags. Just like my fur, isn't it?"

Keeping cosy

"You don't have to go to the polar regions to enjoy snuggling up. I'm just an ordinary domestic cat, and I like nothing better than to curl up and have a nice long nap. By sleeping curled up I can maintain the ideal body temperature, and I don't have to worry about the cold."

Cold? Snuggle up...

"We penguins are social creatures. In the coldest days of the year we gather as a colony and huddle together. We keep our youngest and weakest at the centre of the huddle, where it is warmest. This delightful snuggling-up is known as social thermoregulation."

Small ears, short tails

Why do Arctic animals have such small ears and short tails? So they don't get frostbitten, of course! The larger the ears, the greater the loss of heat from the animal's body. Their legs have a special mechanism to prevent heat loss, too. And that's not all – the overall temperature of Arctic animals' legs is much lower than other parts of their bodies. This allows them to walk on ice without their paws feeling cold. Lucky things! Most Arctic animals are so perfectly adapted for life in the cold that they would not survive in warmer conditions. Remember the mammoth...?

Frost, snow, plants and insects...

How do plants survive periods of snow, ice and cold wind? Whereas animals can walk away, hibernate or go to warmer places, plants have no choice but to stay where their roots are. One of the worst things about winter for plants is that most water is frozen. They can't take in water that has turned to ice.

Plants in a polar world

Flowers grow in infertile polar regions, too. Trees grow low to the ground or in shapes best suited to the snow that bombards them. Plants retain their dead leaves for insulation against the cold.

Honeybee

"Buzzzz… I'm a hard-working honeybee and you can find me in Greenland. Here and there a flower will blossom, and I pollinate it and collect honey. I must go – I'm warmer when I fly!"

Naked in winter

Plants have found their own solution to the shortage of water in winter by shedding their leaves. Leaves tend to cause water to evaporate, so trees shed their leaves and become inactive. The leaves of evergreen plants acquire a thick, waxy coat, which guards against loss of water.

11

People and snow

Three cheers for sledging!

Sledging is great fun! Did you know that sledging is a proper sports discipline called bobsledding? The competitor lies on the sledge, steering it by their body movements alone.

It's snowing – hurray! Let's build a snowman or have a snowball fight! Snow is loved by grown-ups and kids alike, especially those who are hooked on winter sports. Or how about some sledging? Just sit down, hold tight and off you go.

The first sledges

The first racing sledges were made in Norway at the beginning of the 19th century. They looked just like children's sledges today. Guess how old the world's very oldest sledge is? A sledge, discovered in Heinola in Finland, dates from about 6500 BCE.

Snowshoes

Snowshoes have helped people walk more easily in the snow since time immemorial. Traditional snowshoes have a wickerwork frame with a latticework sole and leather bindings to attach them to the feet.

Animals lead the way

Guess how people got the idea of snowshoes? They realised that animals with larger feet could run better on the snow, so they made their own feet bigger by creating snowshoes.

Snowboards and airboards

A snowboarder's feet are both secured to the board while riding the snow. Airboarders use a lilo with two handles. An airboard is light – and when deflated, it fits easily into a rucksack.

Downhill or cross-country?

Sledging tends to be people's first experience of sliding through snow. Grownups usually swap their sledges for skis. The skis used to go downhill are called downhill skis. Cross-country skis, on the other hand, are for travelling across winter landscapes.

snowboard

It's great fun on ice

There are so many activities that we can do on ice – sliding, skating, ice-dancing, speed-skating, hockey…

airboard

Waiting for snow to fall?

Winter sports are enjoyed by many people. But what happens if no snow falls? They have to make their own artificial snow!

The downside of snow cannons

Snow cannons are noisy! They frighten wild animals in the area, especially at night. What's more, they consume huge amounts of electricity and water. They are not at all friendly to the environment.

Artificial snow

Artificial snow is man-made. Just like real snow, it is composed of water and air. Snow-making machines, or snow cannons, spray artificial snow across ski slopes so people can enjoy skiing.

How do snow cannons work?

Snow cannons fire great quantities of snow onto ski slopes. How do they work? They atomize water mist into a stream of supercooled air, which freezes as snow. However, the air temperature needs to be low enough for the snow cannons to work. Artificial snow is created when there is a shortage of snow, or to top up bare areas of ski slopes.

A-va-laaaanche!

An avalanche is a sudden huge rush of snow down a slope. When a thick mass of snow slides down a mountainside, it gathers speed and strength as it falls and can wipe away anything in its path. Avalanches can be caused by significant warming, by a heavy frost or a heavy fall of fresh snow. They can also be started by a passing skier, a helicopter overhead or a loud noise.

Help!

What happens if you lose your way in snow-covered mountains or get caught in an avalanche? The mountain rescue service will come to your aid. They have expert knowledge of all snow and ice conditions and excellent first-aid skills.

Avalanche types

Avalanches of fine, powdery snow spread and endanger areas beyond their main flow. Avalanches of heavy snow are dangerous because their weight and composition can bring rocks down with them, too. Avalanches of ice are equally dangerous.

Cornices

A cornice is a ledge of snow that extends over the edge of a mountaintop. As no one knows when it might fall away, never, ever try to walk onto a snow cornice!

Snow patches

Snow patches can affect roads surrounded by flat fields or meadows. After a heavy fall of snow, a snowplough clears the road by moving the snow to the sides. If the wind gets up, it then blows the snow onto the roads, creating dangerous patches for motorists.

Land of eternal snow and ice

Arctic

Antarctica

Earth has two poles – the North Pole and the South Pole. The polar regions are the coldest places in the world. They never face the Sun. In winter it is dark there for almost 24 hours of each day – this is known as the polar night. In summer the sun shines at all times of day; this is the polar day.

North Pole – the Arctic

The Arctic is not a continent – it is the name we give to the region within the Arctic Circle, an imaginary line around the North Pole. Most of the Arctic consists of the Arctic Ocean, a huge body of water filled with icebergs and solid masses of thick ice. Brrrr...

Arctic environment

The Arctic tundra is covered in snow. Sometimes strong winds whip up the Arctic snow, causing powerful snowstorms which last for several days. The Arctic is a vast white frozen wasteland, where the conditions are very inhospitable: there is little food and, in winter, very little light. The Arctic winter temperatures range between -40 °C and +3 °C; in summer, temperatures can reach the balmy heights of +10 °C.

A Kingdom of ice

Where? In Greenland, of course! In order to visit Greenland, you have to fly over the greatest ice sheet in the Northern Hemisphere. Then you discover fjords filled with blocks of ice. One of these fjords is a perfect glacier, which explains why it is called Icefjord.

South Pole – the Antarctic

The Antarctic is the region around the South Pole which includes the continent Antarctica. This is truly a polar region of eternal ice and darkness. The climate is extremely cold and extremely dry. On average, winter temperatures range between -40 and -70 °C and has been recorded as low as -90 °C. Summer temperatures hover between -10 and -40 °C. The Antarctic mainland is covered with a vast sheet of ice, which forms the majority of the world's fresh-water supply.

The Inuit made short work of winter

The Inuit people are found in Canada, Greenland, Alaska and Siberia – all fiercely cold places with lots of ice. Traditionally, they lived through summer in tents made of animal skins, and they built igloos or dug dwellings in the ground in winter. They kept warm by wearing coats made from the thick fur of reindeer or polar bears. They also wore anoraks — waterproof jackets made out of animal gut – when kayaking.

Take the very best survival equipment available. Wear layers of clothing so you can add or remove layers as required.

Expeditions to the Arctic Circle

Whether a tourist, a scientist or an adventurer, you would have to contend with temperatures way below freezing, permanently frozen ground, ice, snow and bitter winds reaching enormous speeds. Although Antarctica is a desolate, barren land, it is dotted with research stations. Research in the Antarctic was launched by Norwegian polar explorer Roald Amundsen, who in 1911 led the very first expedition to the South Pole.

Mind your head

In polar regions, your face and body extremities will suffer most in the freezing conditions. It is vital that your head and face and your hands and feet are well protected.

Scientific research

Polar scientists take samples, examine microbes and monitor the effects of extreme conditions on humans. They also study glacier activity and observe polar animals and fish. They measure every aspect of this inhospitable region.

Food and Travel

What about food? Mmm… great news for lovers of chocolate. You will need lots of energy, so fill your rucksack with chocolate bars – or better still, fill your sledge (as long as you can still pull it!).

Snow-free places

There are some places in the world where snow never falls. But artificial snow can be created as a substitute.

For all abilities!

Different colour-coded pistes provide skiing for a range of abilities. Beginners can attend a ski school with professional instructors. Imagine sitting on a ski lift in the middle of the desert. Amazing!

Skiing in the desert

Everything is possible! Even a country beset by great heat and red-hot sands can have its own ski area now. A snow dune in the middle of the desert? How extraordinary!

Desert snowballs

There's a huge interest in snow in Dubai, an extremely hot country in the Middle East. In 2005, an enormous indoor ski resort was created, complete with ski slopes, toboggan runs, trees and ski lifts - all built in the desert!

Now that's a good idea

People always want more! Skiing in the desert? That's easy. But can we make snow fall from the sky? In some parched areas they are planning to make artificial snow that falls from the sky. The snow will be produced by machines and special cooling pipes will be installed below ground level so it doesn't melt as it lands.

Snow as a building material

It was the Eskimos who built houses out of snow, called igloos. The first European to see a real, authentic igloo was English explorer Martin Frobisher, when he visited the Canadian Arctic in the 16th century.

Mini-igloo

Can you imagine sleeping under the stars in Antarctica? Brrr ... it's so cold you wouldn't live to see the morning. So hunters build temporary mini-igloos. They can make one quickly in about thirty minutes.

Winter is never boring

The Inuit people of Greenland built spacious halls out of ice. There they could pass the long winter evenings dancing, singing and enjoying wrestling competitions.

Welcome to our igloo

A medium-sized, one-room igloo is perfect for a young married couple. A large igloo with tunnels leading to smaller ones is more suitable for a large family that needs more space.

Snow and heat

It must be cold inside an igloo, surely? No, because snow is a great insulator. The temperature inside can be 60 degrees higher than the temperature outside. The warmth inside the igloo causes the snow to melt a bit, but once empty, it freezes again. This ongoing cycle of melting and freezing turns the ice inside the igloo as hard as concrete.

The best snow for igloos

What kind of snow is best for igloo-building? The kind of snow that is so hard and compacted that you don't leave footprints in it. This type of snow is perfect for cutting into blocks.

How to build an igloo

You will need blocks of snow to build an igloo. The joints are polished so that they fit together. There's no need for mortar or cement. The roof can bear the weight of a grown man. There is a small hole in the roof for ventilation. The entrance to the igloo is below ground level so the heat stays inside as though in a bubble. Cold air has practically no way of getting in, so snuggle up!

why is an igloo dome-shaped?

Well, it looks good... but that's not the main reason. The dome shape is so well-balanced that it can withstand the strongest winds on the northern plains. Perfect, isn't it?

Tourism in the snow and ice

So you think igloo life is only for the Eskimos? Think again – you too can stay in a house made of snow and ice. In Finland you can book into an ice hotel.

How do Finns build ice roofs?

In Finland, they build dome-shaped roofs by inflating a large balloon and covering it with snow. When the snow freezes, the balloon is deflated, leaving a perfect hemisphere. Easy!

Ice hotels

In Finland, when November comes around, people start building the ice hotels. Snow cannons are used to put artificial snow into iron moulds, until it gradually freezes. This creates big building blocks to build the ice rooms, which are then joined together by snow corridors.

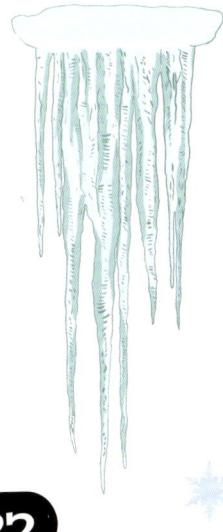

Brrr... an icy bedroom?

Not only is ice good for thermal insulation, it's great for soundproofing, too. Sleeping in an ice room means that you don't hear a peep – there's absolute silence. The beds are made of ice, too, but they are covered with rubber mattresses and thick furs.

The end of the season...

The ice-hotel season lasts until about the middle of April. Ice hotels close when the first thaw arrives. It's no fun having puddles in your room and getting dripped on at night. The hotels are simply left to melt. So ice hotels often just drain back into the lake or river nearby which supplied the water to make the artificial snow in the first place.

Ice and snow art

Artists, too, are inspired by the pure crystal charm of ice. They carve fabulous sculptures out of transparent blocks, even though their work will not survive beyond the winter.

Ice kingdoms really do exist!

During the winter months, Harbin, the coldest city in China, is home to the most famous festival of snow and ice sculptures. Harbin's visitors are entranced by wonders such as the palace of the Snow Queen, life-size ships, fairy-tale princesses and much more.

Ice-sellers

Did you know that there are companies that produce and sell transparent blocks of ice? Drinking glasses and dishes are made from ice, too! There are 19 different types of ice in the world, so perhaps it can be put to more use still?

Making an ice sculpture

1. Freeze a plastic tub of water.
2. Draw a simple sketch.
3. Take the frozen block from the freezer.
4. Carve out your sculpture.

When ice gets in the way

Rather than making things with ice, we sometimes demolish it. When people really need to get across it, an icebreaker is put into action. An icebreaker is a ship that clears the way for other vessels.

Snow and ice everywhere

Brrr... after all this talk of snow and ice, you must be feeling a bit chilly. But I think we can squeeze in some more ice-inspired thoughts, don't you?

The two sides of ice and snow

Snow and ice can be such fun. You can have a great time skating, having snowball fights, building a snowman or an igloo... But when it gets really cold, it can cause frostbite and can even freeze people to death.

A fateful collision

Ice was responsible for the sinking of the Titanic. It was the largest, most luxurious ocean-going liner of its time and was supposed to be unsinkable. On 14 April 1912 at 11.40pm exactly, the liner collided with an iceberg. Less than three hours later, the Titanic sank to the seabed, having failed to complete its first voyage. More than 1,500 passengers and crew were lost.

Careful, it's slippery!

Icy pavements can cause havoc. Hard falls can be painful and often result in broken bones.

Abominable Snowman

Lone pilgrims travelling through the Himalayas have claimed to have seen the Abominable Snowman, or Yeti. Although this creature resembles a human, it is said to be three metres tall. It is bearded and covered in soft animal hair. An incredibly agile climber, the Abominable Snowman can run faster than a horse and swim faster than a motor boat.

Yeti magic

The Abominable Snowman is said to have magical abilities. Terrorised dogs, unable to bark, run from it in horror. Yeti sightings have been recorded over many years and there are those who believe that it comes from another planet.

Scientists and the Yeti

Scientists who have examined and analysed hair samples said to be from the Abominable Snowman say they come from the Himalayan brown bear. The mysterious Yeti story is more fascinating though, isn't it?

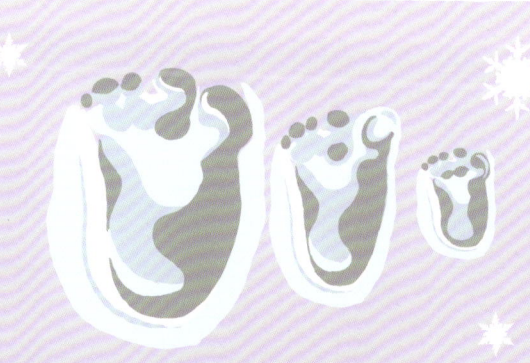

Types of Yeti

The people of the Himalayas, who are convinced of the Yeti's existence, have identified three types of Abominable Snowman – small, large and huge. How? From their footprints, of course.

Snow on Mars

Sometimes snow also falls on Mars. But this is dry snow, not the kind we know on Earth. It's formed from carbon dioxide, not ice. (Humans exhale carbon dioxide and plants turn it back into oxygen.) Just as the red planet has dry snow, it also has dry ice – meaning that Martians, too, can skate, ski and build snowmen!

Snow that puts out fires

Carbon dioxide is the main ingredient of the special snow used in fire extinguishers. A burst of this fire-quenching snow puts out fires caused by electrical equipment or flammable gases or liquids. The temperature of the special snow foam is -78 °C. Brrr!

Edible snow

You can find snow that doesn't feel cold and tastes delicious in the kitchen. Anyone who can whisk egg whites can make it... In some languages, the solid yet fluffy stuff that you know as meringue is called snow. If you mix it with sugar and leave it in the oven to dry out slowly, you'll make yourself a delicious dessert.

A sweet ending

Now that really is everything. Why not join me for a meringue and some hot tea? Look at my frozen hands and red nose. Don't laugh, though – you're not much better off!

Glossary

Brothers Grimm
German brothers who became famous for their collections of folktales gathered from villages across Germany.

Continent
One of the larger continuous bodies of land: Africa, Antarctica, Asia, Australia, Europe, North America and South America.

Eskimo
Groups of people native to the Arctic and subarctic regions.

Finland
A country in northern Europe, between Russia and Sweden, covered in snow and thick woodland.

Hexagon
A six-sided geometric shape.

Humidity
The amount of water vapour in the atmosphere at a particular location.

Kayak
A type of canoe used by Eskimo peoples, with a light frame and a small hole in the top to sit in.

Transparent
A material through which light can pass, allowing objects to be seen through it.

Index

Published in Great Britain in MMXVIII by
Book House, an imprint of
The Salariya Book Company Ltd
25 Marlborough Place, Brighton BN1 1UB
www.salariya.com

ISBN: 978-1-912006-83-0

SALARIYA

1 3 5 7 9 8 6 4 2

© Designed by B4U Publishing, 2016
A member of Albatros Media Group
Author: Štěpánka Sekaninová
Illustrations: Niké Papadopulosová
www.b4upublishing.com
All rights reserved.
Translation rights arranged though JNJ Agency, Texas Allen
English text © The Salariya Book Company Ltd MMXVIII

A CIP catalogue record for this book is available
from the British Library.

Printed and bound in China.